# *NSDQ*

a Night Stalkers CSAR romance story

by

M. L. Buchman

Published by Buchman Bookworks

This title was originally published in the anthology *Way of the Warrior* by Sourcebooks, Inc.


Discover more by this author at:
www.mlbuchman.com

Cover images:
U.S. Army UH-60 Black Hawk helicopter © Michael Kaplan | Wikimedia Commons
Lighthouse Searchlight Beam Through Marine Air At Night © Dreamer82 | Dreamstime.com

# Other works by M.L. Buchman

## The Night Stalkers

### Main Flight

*The Night Is Mine*
*I Own the Dawn*
*Wait Until Dark*
*Take Over at Midnight*
*Light Up the Night*
*Bring On the Dusk*
*By Break of Day*

### White House Holiday

*Daniel's Christmas*
*Frank's Independence Day*
*Peter's Christmas*
*Zachary's Christmas*
*Roy's Independence Day*

### and the Navy

*Christmas at Steel Beach*
*Christmas at Peleliu Cove*

### 5E

*Target of the Heart*
*Target Lock on Love*

## Firehawks

### Main Flight

*Pure Heat*
*Full Blaze*
*Hot Point*
*Flash of Fire*

**Smokejumpers**

*Wildfire at Dawn*

*Wildfire at Larch Creek*

*Wildfire on the Skagit*

**Delta Force**

*Target Engaged*

*Heart Strike*

**Angelo's Hearth**

*Where Dreams are Born*

*Where Dreams Reside*

*Maria's Christmas Table*

*Where Dreams Unfold*

*Where Dreams Are Written*

**Eagle Cove**

*Return to Eagle Cove*

*Recipe for Eagle Cove*

*Longing for Eagle Cove*

*Keepsake for Eagle Cove*

**Deities Anonymous**

*Cookbook from Hell: Reheated*

*Saviors 101*

**Dead Chef Thrillers**

*Swap Out!*

*One Chef!*

*Two Chef!*

**SF/F Titles**

*Nara*

*Monk's Maze*

*The Me and Elsie Chronicles*

*Newsletter signup at:*
*www.mlbuchman.com*

# 1

***US Army Captain Lois*** Lang circled her Black Hawk helicopter five miles outside the battle zone and ten thousand feet up. Usually height equaled safety in countries like Afghanistan where the Taliban had no air power, especially in the middle of the night. Get above the reach of most of the cheaper weapons—rifles, rocket-propelled grenades, and the like—and you were generally safe.

But the Lataband Pass, visible as a thousand shades of green in her night-vision gear, deep in the heart of the Hindu Kush Mountains, was at eight thousand feet and the surrounding peaks cleared ten easily. Even at night in the mountains, ten thousand was pushing the high-hot limit of the helicopters. The high altitude and mid-summer temperatures gave her helicopter's rotor blades thinner air to push against. To get higher, she'd have to really burn fuel; never a good bet on a long mission.

So, she and her crew circled wide and low, and watched their threat displays closely. Not a soul this far from the pass, not even a goatherd. Nothing to do but wait. Their job was CSAR—she always thought of a seesaw whenever she heard the acronym for Combat Search and Rescue, every time—which meant their night would be quiet and routine, unless something went wrong with the attack the US Army's 160th was about to unleash at the heart of the pass.

A ground team, probably from the 75th Rangers, had been dumped in this barren wasteland a week before to do recon. And for tonight, they'd reported a massive convoy of munitions crossing this disused pass from Jalalabad, Pakistan, to supply the Taliban forces inside Afghanistan. With the draw-down of US troops, the Taliban were gearing up to hit the Afghani government forces and hit them hard. Special Ops Forces' job tonight was to make sure the Talies didn't receive the supplies from the ever-so-innocent Pakistanis.

"Keeping chill?" she asked her crew.

"Chill," Dusty replied from his copilot's seat beside her. He'd been a backender, only recently jumped from a back-seat gunner crew chief to front-seat copilot, and they were rotating him through the different helos for cross-training. He normally flew troop transport but had logged time in the heavy weapons DAP version of the Black Hawk, as well. Now that it was nearing his last flight in CSAR, she'd definitely miss him. It was tradition to scoff at backenders who aspired to be pilots, but Dusty definitely had what it took.

"We be very cool, Superwoman," Chuff and Hi-Gear answered from their crew chief positions right behind the pilots' seats.

Her nickname had been inevitable. Being named for both of Superman's girlfriends, Lois Lane and Lana Lang, had labeled her for life. Her mother had always been a crack up, right to her last comment from her death bed, "Flying out now, honey." The fact that Lois had the same light build, narrow face, and straight dark hair as Margot Kidder—who'd played Lois in the old *Superman* movies—didn't help matters.

The two crew chiefs sat in back-to-back seats facing sideways out either side of the helicopter. Steerable M134 miniguns were mounted right in front of them.

The days of the UH-1 Huey medical helos with the big white square and red cross painted on their unarmed bellies were long gone. Bad guys now thought the red crosses made for good targets. And in the modern world of strike-and-retreat tactics, there was no quiet after-the-battle moment when it would be safe to go in and gather the wounded.

Rescue ops now happened right in the heart of the fray, and a medical helicopter arrived ready to both save lives and deliver death simultaneously. Some of the old-guard guys complained about that but not SOAR. The 160th Special Operations Aviation Regiment had flown into Takur Ghar, bin Laden's compound, and a thousand other hellholes, and CSAR crews like hers had been there to pull the lead crews back out when things went bad.

The two medics, a couple of new guys, checked in with her as well. They were the real crazies: Chuck and Noreen. They went into a hot battle zone armed with a stretcher and a medical bag. Beyond crazy.

"Thirty seconds," she called as the mission clock continued counting down to 0200. The Night Stalkers, as everyone called the 160th SOAR, ruled the night. "Death Waits in the Dark" was their main motto, and they did. They were the most highly trained helicopter pilots in any military, and she'd busted her ass for eight years to fly with them, spent two more years in training, and had now been in the air with them for two more. It was her single finest achievement.

Even five miles out, the flash of the first strike was a clear streak across the infrared night-vision image projected on her helmet's visor. The resulting explosion was small. The night's mission brief had said to stop the convoy, gather intelligence, then destroy the munitions. So, first strike had been merely to stop the gunrunners' forward progress and get their attention.

The latter part definitely worked. Fire raked

skyward and not just little stuff. She could see anti-aircraft tracers arcing upward in a white-hot trail of glowing phosphors and hoped that no one was in the way.

"Stay sharp," she warned herself and her crew. The fire show was a distraction for others to worry about. Their worry was—

"CSAR 4. Immediate extract. Grid 37," Archie, the air mission commander called in. He was back at their helibase a hundred miles into Pakistan, watching their world from an MQ-1C Gray Eagle drone circling another fifteen thousand feet above them.

She acknowledged and dove for the dirt roadway. Grid 37 was right in the gut of the pass, so coming in high was just asking for trouble with the on-going battle she could see still in progress. At five feet above Lataband Pass, she unleashed the five thousand horse-power of the twin GE turbine engines. Fifteen thousand pounds of Black Hawk helicopter flung itself toward the battle at two hundred miles an hour. Even with the twists and turns of the narrow gravel road winding between the steep peaks, they were just two minutes out.

These were always the fastest and the

slowest two minutes of her life. At her present altitude and the narrow valley she was flying in, even a stray boulder was a life-threatening hazard. Constant adjustments were needed to crest every rise and take advantage of every little dip. This is what SOAR trained for: flying nap-of-the-Earth to come out of nowhere, in the dead of night, exactly on target and on time.

Yet every second that ticked by, someone lay on the battlefield fighting to stay alive long enough to be rescued. She drove the turbines another couple RPMs closer to yellow-line on the engine's tachometers.

This time the faster feeling won out, and they were on the battlefield with a shocking abruptness. And battle was definitely the operative word. Her tactical display showed two Black Hawks and two of the vicious Little Birds dancing across the sky. But there had been three Little Bird helicopters when they left the airbase.

Grid 37.

Pulling back on the cyclic control to right between her knees for a hard flare dumped speed. Pulling up on the collective along the left side of her seat gained just enough altitude to keep her tail rotor out of the dirt as she slowed. She hammered them down less than a hundred feet from the crumpled remains of the Little Bird helicopter.

Everything was happening at once. Chuff and Hi-Gear were already laying down covering fire, their miniguns blazing with a dragon's deep-throated roar. At three thousand rounds a minute, they scorched the earth anywhere they spotted a bad guy. Chuck and Noreen were already out at a dead sprint toward the crumpled helo.

She debated pulling back aloft to offer them better cover, but the intensity of the overhead air battle told her if she went aloft, she'd have to move well out of the area to be of any use. Her people stood a better chance if she stayed on the ground.

So instead, she remained a sitting duck in the heart of Grid 37 and counted the seconds. A hundred-foot sprint, with heavy gear but high adrenaline: ten seconds. If the injured weren't trapped but perhaps delirious enough with pain to fight against rescue: thirty seconds to get them strapped down. A hundred-foot return carrying deadweight on a stretcher or slow-limping someone back to her aircraft: twenty seconds more. If they were bloody lucky, they only had to survive one minute beneath the tracer-lit madness so close above them.

Rather than watch the medics, she watched the tactical displays. She was getting heavy cover from above. A technical appeared from nowhere around an outcrop: a Toyota pickup with a heavy-caliber machine gun mounted on the bed—serious nightmare vehicle. But Hi-Gear was on it, and in moments the truck was adding its own fireball plume to the light and confusion of the night.

"Ten," one of the medics shouted.

Lois shifted from counting up seconds—she'd only reached forty so they were ten full seconds ahead of her best estimate—to counting them down. She eased up on the collective until the helicopter was dancing on the dirt in its eagerness to be aloft.

She ignored the bright sparks of bullets pinging off her forward windscreen, hoping nothing was a big enough caliber to punch through. Her audio-based threat detector filling her ears with muted squeals indicating only small-arms fire; the big stuff was still hunting the SOAR attackers overhead. The directional microphones translated each bullet's trajectory into fire-return data, and her crew chiefs were pounding back on those positions.

At five seconds to go, a crowd came out of the roiling dust kicked up by her rotors.

She glanced over for just an instant and then returned her attention to tactical while her mind unraveled what she'd just seen. One medic carrying a man over his shoulder, dead-man style. The second medic pulled one end of a stretcher, the other end dragging on the road's gravel surface with a body strapped to it; good, both of her crew accounted for. Two other guys limping in with their arms around each others' shoulders, clearly nothing else keeping them upright.

The last two deserved a second glance. MICH helmets and HK416 rifles rather than the FN SCARs that all of SOAR carried across their chests. Delta Force operators. If Delta were on the ground here, it meant this action was much heavier duty than she'd thought.

That explained the unexpected scale of the firefight.

At zero on her countdown, she could feel the shift in her two-inch high hover as the team slammed aboard. She gave the stretcher bearer an extra three seconds to load.

The "GO!" came just as she racked up on the collective getting her off the dirt and airborne without a wasted instant.

Whatever was happening in the cargo bay was no longer her problem. They could do everything that most field hospitals could do. If you were alive when CSAR got you, your life expectancy was very high. And sometimes even if you weren't.

Lois punched through the dust brownout kicked up by her own rotors and headed back the way she'd come. She slewed hard to clear the first turn in the road as the battle behind her moved toward the other end of the pass.

She climbed enough to keep her rotor blades clear of the ground and leaned into the first turn in the ravine.

She barely had time to see the white-hot streak coming in her direction. "RPG!" the warbling tone of the threat detector screeched out. The rocket-propelled grenade impacted her Number One turbine engine with no chance of an evasive maneuver. Dusty pulled the overhead Fire Suppress T-handle as Chuff's minigun announced he was taking care of whoever had gotten them. That was no longer the problem.

The problem was she was in a turn that needed four-thousand horsepower to recover from, and she now had twenty-six hundred. She cranked the Number Two engine right into redline and yanked up hard on the collective.

Not enough. The steep rock wall of the pass loomed before them. The night-vision gear gave her a perfect, crystalline view—as well-lit as if it were broad daylight—of the boulder field that was going to kill her Hawk.

And her crew. No! There!

Normally, she'd yank back on the cyclic and let the tail hit first and then belly-flop the bird down—worked well on a flat landing area. The Hawk could take a lot of abuse that way and could often be bounced off its wheels and they'd be on their way.

But not with these boulders. The very worst of the damage path would be right through the center of the cargo bay where she had four injured, two medics, and two crew chiefs.

She slammed over the cyclic and rammed down hard on the right rudder pedal, intentionally driving the pilot's side rotor blade into the cliff wall.

They would tumble in a hard roll, but it offered the best chance of the crew's survival.

Only one problem.

She'd known it even before she'd slammed over the controls but didn't shy away.

US Army Captain Lois Lang's position was the very first point of contact in the developing crash.

# 2

***Lois jerked awake in*** a cold sweat.

No cockpit!

Crisp white sheets. Soft pillow.

She let out a long, slow sigh of relief. If the damn dream insisted on waking her every single morning, why did it have to be so utterly accurate? And real. Her adrenaline was through the roof, her heart rate only now cascading down through stratospheric flight levels.

She was in her own apartment in Fort Lewis post housing. She was still here, housed with the rest of the SOAR 5th Battalion. Like most single soldiers in post housing, her possessions were not a major burden. Most of them were hanging on the white walls: the line of pictures of people she'd served with, the ones she'd dragged out of hell and the pictures of them back in the air or back with their families, and most importantly her different crews over the years—the ones she'd shed blood and sweat with. Her ROTC graduation certificate and the letter signed by the president to commission her as an officer in the US Special Operations Forces were framed at the center of the wall. She belonged here.

At least this time she'd woken before the final crash, which she typically relived in agonizingly slow motion. She'd count that as a good start to the day.

She swung up to a sitting position and stared at her options. Start the day on crutches or crutches with the prosthetic. She wanted to ignore the damn foot, but reminded herself that *Night Stalkers Don't Quit*. NSDQ was a motto commonly heard throughout the regiment during tough times, and she'd been saying it a lot lately. Well, if they didn't quit, that also meant they didn't shy away from the hard choices.

Fine. As of this moment, no matter what the medicos said, she was done with the crutches. She reached for the foot and began putting it on.

Two layers of anti-abrasion sock that rolled up over her knee, at least *that* was still hers. She'd always been told she had great legs, had enjoyed wearing shorts to the inevitable volleyball or beach gatherings to show them off. Now, not so much.

She slid on the socket and strapped it into place. She'd tried the suction mount but never liked the slick feel of it. So, socks and straps. They'd offered her two different right-foot prostheses, but she'd only taken the one. She didn't need some dandied-up version of cosmesis. Her right foot was gone; a transtibial shear-off right at mid-calf as she'd kept the rudder pedal rammed down throughout the entire crash to buy every last ounce of safety she could for her crew. And it had worked. Other than a few broken ribs and a concussion, hers was the only injury. If she had to deal with a false foot, then people would have to accept her as she was.

For the first time since the crash, she didn't

pull on pants, but chose a skirt instead. *If you're gonna do it, girl, you're gonna do it all the way.* So, no false camouflage either.

The leg came with a fake, skin-toned covering shaped like a human foot. For a long moment she considered throwing that in the garbage disposal for good measure, but it would just clog the thing up. Hell, lettuce would clog her damned disposal. She chucked the offending plastic covering—with its fake big-toe gap so she could wear a sandal—in the garbage. She had a custom sneaker that would hide most of the prosthetic's mechanics, but she bypassed that as well, opting to clip on just the rubber toe and heel pads that left the mechanical foot exposed.

They'd released her from the WTU yesterday. Thank goodness Joint Base Lewis-McChord had one of the Warrior Transition Units right on the base. That meant she'd been able to go through much of her recovery in her own apartment. Well, if the WTU had decided to declare her healthy, then she'd start acting healthy.

She was still awkward without the crutches. Once dressed, she walked back and forth across the apartment several times. With a curse, she assessed herself as not stable enough to go out without at least a cane. She'd long since discovered just how badly it hurt when she took an unexpected tumble, and this wasn't a good day for that.

They'd promised that this foot with its aluminum core and titanium fittings was solid and durable enough for her to run on, but she still found that hard to credit.

The nerve sensations she received from her missing foot had nothing to do with what her new one was doing. She actually did better if she didn't keep looking down to see when it was on the ground and when it was in the air, but it was hard to break the habit when she couldn't actually feel the ground. Every step was a surprise when ground contact actually occurred—especially because she felt it in her calf and knee, not her foot.

At the door, she really, really wished she didn't have to hold onto the knob for a good ten minutes before she could force herself to go through, but she did. That, too, was part of her new reality.

Head finally high, she made it out the door

and through the small lobby. Thankfully, she'd had a ground floor unit, as the complex had no elevators. Refusing the ADA-compliant access ramp, between her cane and the railing she did manage the three steps out front. The Medical Evaluation Board offices were only a half mile away. She could have called for a car, but for a woman used to twenty-mile runs, it was too demeaning.

*NSDQ. NSDQ.*

Summer had given way to fall in the Pacific Northwest while she'd recovered. The blazing arid heat of the high passes of the Hindu Kush would be switching to freezing temperatures and impassible snow.

Snow was rare here at Lewis-McChord, but she could smell that fresh snap left by an overnight rain, which would be snow atop the nearby fourteen-thousand-foot peak of Mount Rainier. The thick smell of evergreen and undertone of moss was unique to the Pacific Northwest. She could practically taste apple cider season on the air and the hint of the ocean from the waters of Puget Sound. The sunlight felt cool as it shone off the wet paving of the walkway. This was home. At least until the Army medically retired her and said it wasn't anymore.

"Hey, Lois. How's life on the *Daily Planet* today?"

"Hey, Clark. Doing just *super*!" And she was doing a little better for Kendall Clark's presence. She'd allowed herself an hour to cross the half mile to the MEB building—and only spent ten minutes of it clutching her doorknob in a desperate search for inner strength—so she could afford to stop and rest a moment after the first hundred yards. "How about you?"

"Super, now that I've run into you." And he really did look super. Always a little standoff-ish but a pleasure to look at.

"Haven't seen you in a bit." Not since before her accident.

"Was at the Sikorsky home office in Connecticut for some upgrade training the last couple months. Didn't know you were back until just yesterday."

"Back." Nice way to put it. Nicest she'd heard yet. Clark was the Black Hawk specialist embedded at Fort Lewis by Sikorsky—the Hawk's manufacturer. Part engineer, part instructor, and all around good egg. It was inevitable that they'd been thrown together, aside from the training he provided. With him being almost the Clark Kent mild-mannered alias of the superhero, it had been inevitable.

Others had picked up on it even before they met. Crazy Tim had started it, of course, going way out of his way to introduce them. Then he'd set off on a quest to find a Jimmy and a Perry to form the "ultimate team against evil." He hadn't reported any results yet. Of course, Crazy Tim was still aloft in Afghanistan, and she was permanently grounded in Washington State, a bitter pill she did her best to spit out rather than swallow.

# 3

***Kendall's eyes kept tracking*** down to Lois's uncovered prosthetic foot. He'd pull them away and look back up at her eyes, but it was clearly giving him trouble.

"It's okay, Clark. I'm going to just have to get used to it." She wasn't happy about it but tried not to sound too upset either, she was the one who'd chosen the skirt after all. "Go ahead, give it the good once over." She leaned on her cane and turned it sideways for him to see.

He squatted down to look, then had the decency to glance back up at her to make sure it was okay. He was such a geek, one of his more charming features. Actually, one of his many charming features. She'd always liked him once Tim had bumped them together.

"The Soleus Tactical," she filled him in. "They designed it specifically for a double amputee named Dale Beatty. National Guard guy who hit an IED over in the Dustbowl." Iraq and Afghanistan lacked many things, but they had plenty of dust. Six months out and she could still feel it clogging her pores.

"Slick. The springs are adjustable?"

It was the first time anyone other than a doctor or physical therapist had even been allowed to see it. If there was anyone to be her "first time," she liked that it was Kendall. For reasons she didn't care to contemplate, she was ridiculously tempted to run her hand through his black hair not so different from Clark Kent's. Was she that desperate for company?

"Yeah," was the answer to both questions. "They keep re-tuning the springs as I get used to it, though they're pretty well done with changes now. The harder I push down, the more reaction back I get. They say I can run on it. That won't be anytime soon, I can promise you. Even with the socket, it weighs less than my real foot. Great weight loss plan, huh?"

The engineer in him came out as he tapped a finger against a couple parts of the armature. It was so personal—almost as if he'd just stroked his hand down her bare foot. She must have reacted somehow, because he suddenly jerked his hand back, looked up at her in shocked apology, and proceeded to tip back onto his butt in an effort to withdraw.

"Crap!" He'd landed on the wet grass, which responded with a distinct squishing sound. Then he looked up at her again. "I'm so sorry. I shouldn't have… Sorry. I wasn't thinking."

He was trying to get up without placing his hands in the mud, as well.

She braced herself and offered her hand to help him up. He took it and, after testing that she could take the load, managed to get back to his feet and stand.

He twisted to inspect the damage, his hand still in hers. She gave his hand a slight tug causing him to expose his wet and muddy behind. He had big hands, good ones. She'd witnessed a thousand times how delicate they were on the controls and how powerful when taking a helicopter apart to inspect it for wear and tear.

"Superman with a wet butt." She could feel the laugh bubbling up inside her. It came out slow and rough. Her voice was long out of practice with making such a sound, but it did come out. She clamped down on it for fear it would go a little hysterical on her. She retrieved her hand, a bit reluctantly. It was her first non-medical contact in six months, and it was surprisingly powerful. So starved for human contact that even clasping hands for a moment had roared through her nervous system and left her jittery. *Pitiful, Lois, really damn pitiful.*

He flexed his hand as if terribly conscious of their contact as well.

"Pretty super move there, Clark," she ribbed him to cover her own unease.

"Damn! I've got a meeting in about twenty minutes. I don't have a change of clothes in the car."

And he lived off post. She remembered a nice party at his house, a bunch of Black Hawk pilots from the 4th and 5th Battalions and a summer's eve barbecue in a suburban backyard.

She and Clark had spent much of the evening chatting quietly beneath the arching branches of an old cherry tree. It was a good memory.

"Here." She dug out her key. "Unit 32. Don't make too much of a mess. Towels and a hair dryer under the bathroom sink. You can bring me the key after your meeting. I'll be over at the MEB offices. Have to do all the Eval Board paperwork about no longer being medically qualified for active duty." She rapped her cane against her foot with a dull clank for emphasis then wished she hadn't.

"Sorry about that, Lois. You were damned good." She had been, but it felt different having the resident Sikorsky guy say it. "Thanks. Real fun begins after they boot me over to the PEB. The Physical Evaluation Board is going to medically retire my ass no matter what I say. You better scoot if you want to make your meeting."

"Right" He held up the key. "Thanks."

"No problem." She turned and began clomping off toward the MEB office. This was not what she planned to be doing with her life. A pair of the big twin-rotor Chinooks lumbered by low overhead, hammering their way aloft on a training flight. That's what she wanted to be doing. Flying. They faded away.

"Hey, Superwoman!" Lois turned at Clark's call and almost ate dirt. Only a quick stab with her cane kept her upright after the unexpected motion.

He should be halfway to the apartment by now, but he still stood where they'd talked; she'd made good a dozen paces from there. He'd been watching her walk like a total Terminator machine, not like the woman she'd once been. She hoped they were far enough apart for him to not see her blush. She kept her chin up so that her embarrassment wouldn't show.

"Unit 32," she told him, risking a point with her cane, the Chinooks moved off enough that she only had to shout a little to be heard. With someone so sharp, he always forgot the strangest things.

"Knew that." He inspected his feet for a moment as if to see if they were prosthetic or as if he didn't want to look at hers.

Fine. She didn't need anyone's symp—

He looked up. "Are you free for dinner tonight?"

"I'm free the rest of my damned life."

"That's a yes then?"

Was she low enough to take a sympathy date? After she was done with the Medical Eval Board, she'd be low enough for anything to look good. It didn't really seem fair to a guy as nice as Kendall to use him to cheer herself up, but he had asked.

"That's a yes."

"Great! I'll get your key back before then." He spun around, stepped off the edge of the concrete walkway, and almost went down in the grass again. Then he righted himself, waved, and rushed off. Odd, he wasn't a clumsy guy, not at all.

Lois turned herself carefully and aimed back along the path. She was surprised to discover that her step was a little lighter than it had been when she started out.

# 4

***"So, did the MEB*** go like you expected?"

Lois looked around the restaurant. She figured they'd grab dinner at the post's mess hall, she'd gather her twenty minutes of sympathy, and he'd be done with her safe in the knowledge he'd performed a kindness. Instead, he'd taken her on a real splurge up to Stanley and Seafort's, perched on the hillside above the city of Tacoma.

First, it was off post—her first time since the crash.

Second, it had an amazing view of the harbor with its big container ships plying the shining waterways of southern Puget Sound. The Olympic Mountains to the west had just gobbled the sun and earned a stunning blood-orange aura for their trouble.

Third, it wasn't the sort of place you had a twenty-minute dinner. It was the sort of place you had a two-hour dinner in nice clothes. She hadn't worn her dress blues or her ACU—Army Combat Uniform—fatigues. Both reminded her too much of the end of her military career, but now she wished she had for the "armor" it would have given her, the explanation of her amputation. Instead, she'd opted for a nice blouse and the same knee-length skirt she'd worn this morning.

Damn Clark for not telling her where they were going. Of course if he had told her, she probably would have balked, and the man wasn't stupid. She hadn't thought to ask, merely hanked her shoulder-length hair back in a ponytail and called it good. Her dog tags were her only ornament, she'd worn those for strength, but with civilian clothes they now felt ridiculous. She slipped them inside her blouse.

Lois wouldn't have minded being dressed

this way on post. Looking like a civilian except for the damned peg leg. But here in public, she really hadn't been ready for the exposure. If only she'd worn slacks, at least the cane alone would be unremarkable. She looked longingly at the exit but didn't want to let Clark down.

She could feel every eye in the place follow her uneven walk to the window table. Not the kind of looks she was used to having follow her across a room. Once seated, the tablecloth was long enough that she felt a little less self-conscious. A little.

"Hello. Lois. Someone hit your hearing with a dose of Kryptonite?"

She tried for a dutiful laugh but had trouble dredging one up.

"I haven't really been off post since…well. It's been a while."

"That's kind of what I figured, thought I'd give you a pleasant night out."

"Well, this is certainly pleasant." White tablecloths, candlelight at each table, immaculate waitress, and a one-page menu that looked so good an additional page would have been overwhelming. Then she glanced at the prices. This was definitely outside a soldier's budget except for something really special. She eyed Kendall suspiciously.

"What?" He closed his menu and set it aside. She could never decide what to get, and he was already done.

"What's going on, Clark? Why are we here?"

He laughed, "You always speak the same way you fly, straight shooter."

"It's what we women of steel do"—she pointed down toward her foot to make her point—"even if we're only partly made of steel. Now, answer the question."

"Actually, I read up on your foot, and it's all aluminum and titanium, so I'm not sure it counts."

"Modern materials, modern woman of steel. Besides, 'woman of aluminum and titanium' doesn't have quite the ring I was looking for when I did this."

He propped his chin on a hand and aimed those dark eyes at her. They caught the candlelight and were warm and friendly.

She resisted the urge to reach out and brush the hair out of his eyes where it had slipped down. What the hell was he doing to her?

"Maybe I just like looking at a beautiful woman while I eat."

"Asked the wrong girl then."

"Says you."

"I'm—" then she stopped herself. The WTU psychologist had given her a list of trigger words to avoid. Words that would be "negative reinforcers for her emotional frame of mind." *Damaged* was way high on the list. She toyed with her water glass to buy some time. The waitress arrived with a long list of memorized specials, which bought her some more time but not enough.

She went with a Dungeness crab-stuffed salmon, Kendall ordered jumbo shrimp and steak.

Damaged.

She had a few other scars besides her leg but nothing hideous. Her foot was far and away the worst of it. Kendall had seen that, inspected it, and still somehow saw her as she'd been before the accident. He made her feel ridiculous for attaching her self-image to something as small as a foot. Well, if he wasn't going to see her that way, maybe she should stop doing so herself. Or at least try.

"Well." She sipped her first glass of wine in a very long time and let the deep red Merlot warm her insides. She circled back to his earlier question as that now seemed to be a much safer topic. "The MEB was about what you'd expect. A lot of paperwork and a lot of sympathy—neither of which I wanted—but because I'm injured past possible recovery to full status, I'm not their problem. Tomorrow, I tackle the Physical Eval Board. That's going to take a while. I really don't want to leave the service, but they're gonna shuffle me out anyway."

"Aren't there plenty of things for you to do?"

"Yeah, great. Army Wounded Warrior program. Talked to the AW2 advocate, but stay in and do what? Fly a desk? The only thing I love to do is fly helos. Well, I sure lost my superpowers on that one."

Kendall reached across the table and took her hand. She let him because it felt so good and it kept the fears at bay.

"There's lots—"

"Let's talk about something else. Anything else."

He squeezed her hand, then he did. Most guys would push and shove. Kendall Clark had apparently decided it was his duty to fly to her rescue and at the moment she wasn't complaining. He started with a funny story from a training mission that somehow involved a standard poodle with the name Underdog and a paper chain of cut-out Santas.

"I swear, I'm not making this up."

She didn't care if he was. As long as he kept holding her hand, she felt as if she somehow belonged.

# 5

***Kendall escorted her to*** her front door. It was long past dark by the time they returned to post. Most of the apartments would be empty, any Night Stalkers not on deployment would be night flying. She found it disorienting to be done with her day while the rest of the company was just starting theirs.

After holding the front door for her and making sure she had her keys, Kendall turned to leave. She was done in, it had been her longest day in a long time, but she still didn't want it to end.

"Hey, Clark. Where are your manners?"

He stopped with one hand on the lobby door and furrowed his brow at her.

"C'mere." She waved him over when he hesitated. He approached cautiously.

"It's rude to hold a woman's hand half the night, tell her she's beautiful when she's feeling like shit, and then you don't at least try for a good night kiss. What's up with that?"

"You want me to kiss you?"

"I wouldn't complain if you at least tried. Don't tell me you haven't been thinking about it." Because she knew *she* had, and it surprised her no end. And not just human-male contact. She wanted some Kendall Clark contact.

He stepped until he was so close that she actually backed up the last half-step against her locked apartment door.

"I…" his voice was soft and deep. They were so close she could feel the vibrations as much from his chest as she could with her ears. "I've been thinking about it since that day two years ago when we sat under the cherry tree in my backyard."

Then, before she could begin to process her shock, he kissed her.

Not some friendly thanks-for-the-nice-date

kiss. Not even a testing kiss from a handsome and geeky guy.

He wrapped his soldier-strong arms around her and pulled her in against his surprisingly hard body. She'd never really quite paid attention to how often he'd joined in when they were doing physical training workouts. Now, she certainly could appreciate that he had. The heat of the kiss built until all she could do was wrap her arms around him and hold on for the ride. And it was a wild one.

He plundered, and she gave until her entire body heated turbine hot. The adrenal roar so loud it drowned out everything except how Kendall felt in her arms, his lips and tongue offering no hint of gentle in their need, and his hands—those wonderful hands—one dug deep into her hair and the other at the small of her back pulling their bodies tight together. Somewhere in the distance she heard the clunk and rattle of her cane falling to the tile floor.

Then, just as abruptly as he'd taken her, he stopped and took a step back. Her hands, so recently clenched in that black wavy hair that was even softer than it looked, now rested on his chest. And his rested comfortably on her waist as if they'd been there a hundred times before.

"Been wanting to do that for a long time, Captain Lang. Even better than I imagined. Way better." He offered a very self-satisfied grin, then kissed her on the tip of the nose. "Sleep well, Superwoman."

He retrieved her cane, slid it into her nerveless fingers, and was gone.

She didn't manage a good-bye or even a wave. Her body buzzed very happily as she let herself into her apartment.

Lois lay down in her bed knowing there was no way she'd find sleep anytime soon. Eight hours later she startled awake—startled because for the first time since the accident, she'd woken up after she'd extracted the injured but before the crash had begun to unfold.

# 6

***Lois spent a grinding*** morning with the Physical Eval Board. All paperwork. "Do you need any help keying this in? No? Okay. Go to computer station B-24 and fill out forms..." and the interminable list had begun. Army thinking, the fact that all the information was on file for the Medical Eval Board didn't mean it was in the right format for the PEB. Thankfully, she'd been smart enough to bring the paper copy of the MEB stuff, so it was mostly transcription.

That had left her plenty of time to think about Kendall while typing. A lot of little pieces began to fit into place. She thought all the way back to that party he'd had out at his place. He knew who he was dealing with so he had some beer, a lot of soda, and an impressive amount of meat for the grill. SOAR pilots were on-call 24-7. They also had a rule of twenty-four hours bottle-to-throttle, so having the chance for a drink didn't happen very often. Some of the ground crew who'd tagged along took a beer, but SOAR was a pretty straight crowd.

But before the party, Kendall had made a point of finding out her preferred beverage. She'd given him two answers, because she could never decide about food. There'd been a significant stock of both the caffeine-free Diet Coke and a giant pitcher of fresh-made iced tea. He'd served her a double cheeseburger on a toasted bun with only stone-ground mustard, without her having to ask. He'd probably gotten that from watching her at cookouts by the hangar and noting that's what she always ate.

With her new perspective of last night's very pleasant memory, that still raised her pulse each time she thought about it, some of the older memories were painting a picture she'd never seen.

So, she sat and remembered and keyed down her family status: none—mother deceased and dad bailed when she was six.

Medical status: BK—below the knee trans-tibial amputation.

Procedure: amputation by five tons of crashing helicopter.

The medics, who had survived the crash mostly intact, had patched her up before she bled out, but it had been a close thing. The hard rattle of gunfire back and forth as Dusty and Hi-Gear guarded their position was a constant backdrop until one of the big DAP Black Hawks had come over and laid down some serious fire from above. Chief Warrant LaRue had really torn up the landscape to protect the downed CSAR craft.

Lois had learned to roll through these flashbacks, offering little outward sign other than a shake of her head to clear it off. Just part of the "new life."

Clara, the one-armed AW2 Advocate, met her for lunch. No, she'd snuck up beside the PEB computer station number B-24 and launched a tactical strike.

Lois could see the woman's determination,

so she rolled with it. But that didn't mean she was above complaining over a BLT.

"I'm getting pretty sick of the 'new life,'" Lois was beyond sick of it. "Where can I put in a requisition for the old one back? Never mind, I know it's not going to happen, but I don't want the new life."

"If you proceed with medical retirement, what are your plans?"

"Well, I sure don't have the patience you're showing in dealing with a jerk like me."

"Then what are your plans?" Clara was tenacious. That's why she hated talking to the advocate. If Lois couldn't fly, she didn't have a clue.

# 7

***"Hey, Superboy." Lois had*** tracked Kendall down in neutral territory. It hadn't been hard. He was usually at the hangars or the simulators, and the simulator building was close enough that she could trust herself to walk there despite the long day at PEB.

"Hey, Woman of Steel. Give me a minute. Got one more run to do."

She considered going up to the controller's console and sitting in the observer's seat, but that felt a little presumptuous, so she found a plastic chair, sat, and propped her cane between her knees.

This glaring white room and its ugly fluorescent lighting was as close to a second home as she had. First was the hangars and sitting in a Black Hawk, but she'd also spent a lot of time in here with the flight simulators. It was a lot cheaper to crash a simulator than a twenty-million-dollar helicopter. They'd cleaned up the remains of her helicopter with a set of destruct charges that left behind nothing bigger than a notepad. Thankfully, she'd been under the drugs by then and hadn't seen her bird go up in a roar of C4 and flames.

The simulator building itself was totally unremarkable. The outside was standard Fort Lewis white with a steel roof. Inside was white-painted concrete. It was the three tall stations that were the whole point. Looking as strange and clunky as two-legged *Star Wars* Imperial scout walkers, the simulators were boxy affairs atop spindly hydraulic pistons a dozen feet high. They allowed the simulator's cockpit to pitch, roll, yaw, and especially buck unexpectedly hard, just like a real helicopter.

Little Bird, Black Hawk, and Chinook—the three helos used by SOAR turned into the three best video games on the planet. She pretended for a moment that everything was normal, and she just sat in the hard plastic chair by the Black Hawk simulator waiting her turn. She tried to recall the casual boredom she must have felt the last time she had sat here, but couldn't find it.

Training was a constant in SOAR. Thousands of hours in flight and thousands more in the trainer. Old Master Sergeant Jake Hamlin had a vicious bent, like he had it in for all SOAR pilots. She used to wonder if he especially had it in for her: flameouts, engine fires, hydraulic failures. All in the midst of a turbulent thunderstorm that had replaced the sunny day on her windscreen just moments before.

Now, all she felt was a loss as some chief warrant she didn't know clambered up into the "box." She should just leave. She really should. But she was tired, her leg—her real one—hurt from being on it all day, and she really did want some words with Kendall. So, she just sat and waited, occasionally looking up when the simulator gave a particularly violent wheeze of hydraulic pistons and a hard lurch. Not a comfortable ride. She closed her eyes and settled in to wait.

"You're up, Missy."

"I wish." Lois smiled even before she opened her eyes to see Jake now standing in front of her. He was as big as Kendall. Despite a couple more decades, he was still Army strong. His hair was now a gray crew cut rather than a salt-and-pepper one like when she'd first met him.

"You're in my chairs, then you're up next. Move your behind, Captain. Your trainer says he's waiting for you." More amused than anything else, she climbed up the steep metal stairs to the simulator's entry level. She could feel Jake close behind her and see that he was carefully gripping the rails on either side. If she stumbled, he'd be braced to catch her. She'd worn slacks today but left the armature exposed. If he had any thoughts about her new foot, he kept them to himself. She made it to the top clean and offered him a nod of thanks for watching out for her.

Kendall was strapped in as left-side copilot. She climbed into the right-side pilot seat, glad she had gone back to pants.

Lois braced for nostalgia, sadness, tears... It had been a long six months since she'd been aboard a Hawk, even a simulated one. Instead, it just felt right. This is where she belonged. Through her thin civilian clothes rather than the normal flightsuit, the seat felt closer, more real, more personal against her body. Not even really thinking about it, she buckled on the harness that lay heavy against her skin through the cotton blouse.

"You remember the way of it?" She ignored Jake's sly comment. Kendall had watched her settle in but hadn't said a word. They traded surreptitious smiles that were just the beginning of a whole conversation they wouldn't be having in front of Jake. She pulled on a headset and adjusted the microphone. Her helmet was in her closet covered with six months of dust, so this would have to do. It felt ridiculously light.

She cycled up the simulator. *One more flight. Just one more.* She didn't bother reaching for the manual, even after six months, the steps of the engine start-up procedure were still a part of her nervous system. The turbines lit off with a simulated roar through her headset.

Falling into his copilot role, Kendall fed her engine temp data and RPMs as she continued down the list flipping the Blade De-icing switch to auto and all the other twenty steps of engine run-up.

The Black Hawk cockpit in the simulator was so real that she could almost believe it, if she weren't in civilian dress. She was the only anomaly in the space. The radio and comm gear ran between her seat and Kendall's, with all the engine controls and electrical system mounted in the ceiling above them. The main console stretched side to side at chest level. At the center, a few key instruments that needed no electricity. Altitude, attitude, and compass would all keep working even if everything else failed. Above them, a large shared screen that might show terrain or weapons status depending on the mission.

In front of Kendall and her were two large glass screens each. The screens had a couple dozen modes so that the displays could be customized as needed. She toggled through the settings using the switch on the collective in her left hand and set up for standard flight information.

Above the console was a wraparound windscreen that showed Fort Lewis airfield, realistically enough to believe she just might be out on the tarmac, sweating in the last heat of the setting sun before a night flight. Down by her feet—foot—was an additional view of the terrain below, just a projection of pavement at the moment. She couldn't feel the right rudder so had to visually check that her foot was on the pedal...it was. She could even get some feel of how much pressure she was applying through her calf and knee. But if she ever wanted to use the brake, she'd have to shift her foot to the top of the pedal to press down—she had no foot to flex.

She called the tower for clearance to depart. Jake Hamlin answered from his control console at the back of the simulator. She eased up on the collective with her left hand and nudged the cyclic forward to get a little nose-down attitude and forward motion. She talked her way out of the flight pattern until she was up over Puget Sound.

Lois was flying. It was only a simulator, but she was up and flying. Her eyes were burning, she had to blink away the incipient tears. She didn't want to brush at her eyes; Kendall would notice when she had him take the collective to free up her hand to do so. Instead, she blinked hard and banked right so that she'd have an excuse to look out the side window away from him. The simulator's pistons canted the cockpit to match her control motions and the video projected on the windows showed the land rotating below her.

Kendall and Jake left her alone and just let her fly. She shook it out a bit, testing her reactions, testing her foot. The control wasn't as bad as she'd feared. The nerve sensations coming up her right leg were different, but she learned to interpret what they were telling her fairly quickly.

Jake threw a small thunderstorm up on the screen, not much more than a squall line, and she climbed for safety and rode out the turbulence. Her gut informed her that her tail rotor control of the rudder pedals wasn't great, but it wasn't bad either. Maybe she could get a civilian job, flying tourists around or something.

After she took them "back to the field," landed, and shut down, she had to just sit there for a long time before she remembered how to breathe. She heard Jake shut down his control station and head down the stairs. When Kendall peeled her left hand off the now inactive collective and held it in his, that's when the pain really began to flow. It took everything she had left in her to keep the tears on the inside.

# 8

***"I lost so much."*** Lois hadn't really been functional after the simulated flight. She'd let herself be led by Kendall. Down the stairs, to his car, back to her apartment. There she'd simply handed him her keys and he let them in.

She'd kept her composure through delivery pizza. Held it together while they spoke of nothing at all really. At least not that she could remember.

"Well, I should—"

"Will you stay?" She could hear his "it's time to leave tone," and she really didn't want to be alone.

Kendall looked at her as if not quite believing what he was hearing.

"Okay, I know I'm a bad bet. I'm"—*to hell with the WTU's words-to-avoid list*—"crippled. I'm an emotional train wreck. And I can't promise I won't be a worse one tomorrow."

"I could sit with you—"

"I'm no longer an invalid in a hospital bed." She stopped herself before it turned into a shout. Getting to her feet, she clomped away from where they'd been sitting ever so carefully on opposite ends of the couch. She came to a stop facing the unlit kitchen, her back to Kendall. Taking a deep breath, she braced her hands on the counter for support but didn't turn as she spoke.

"I've been thinking about what you said. You've been stuck in my head the whole damn day. I finally get that you liked me..."—she thought about last night's dinner and kiss—"like me. I don't know why you never said anything. I can't figure that part out. I was single. I never slept around in the unit or much outside it. Why two years—"

"Because you flew." Kendall had come up behind her without her noticing. His voice was barely a whisper. So close she could feel him there now, though he didn't touch her.

"Because I flew?" But that's everything she was…had been. "You didn't clue me in about how you felt, because I flew."

"Yes."

She spun to face him so fast that he took a quick step back. "Oh, but now that I can't fly, now that the sky has been ripped away from me, now it's okay to kiss me like you want to take me to bed? Well, to hell with you." She tried to storm away, but he stopped her. He was far more powerful than she was, could have caged her against the counter, done anything, and she couldn't have stopped him.

All Kendall did was rest his hand lightly on her arm and suddenly all of her momentum failed her.

"Why?" She couldn't look up to meet those dark eyes. "Can you at least tell me why?"

He nodded slowly, then led her back to the couch. His hand was strong and warm as he supported her through the still awkward transition from standing to sitting. She wanted to curl her legs under her, but the metal creeped her out when it brushed her other leg.

"It's not that you flew—"

"But you just said—"

He held up his hand to stop her. His face was unreadable. She might not remember much of their last hour together, but she had remembered watching the mobility of his features. His easy smile, the laugh that started in his eyes long before it reached his lips or his voice. There was something behind his eyes now, a darkness she recognized and now wished she didn't. Kendall had become her beacon of light somewhere along the way. Two dinners and a kiss hadn't been what did it.

The flight. The gift of flight, even if it was a simulated one. She couldn't see where the hope led, but she could feel it lying somewhere just out of reach.

Well, the light had gone out, and now the man sitting across from her was frowning with a seriousness she didn't recognize, didn't know he had in him.

"My dad flew Desert Storm." His voice with thick and slow. "He's one of the ones who didn't make it home."

"I'm so sorry." She reached out and took his hand. Why hadn't she known? Because he hadn't told her, *duh*! But as she watched how hard it was, she understood that not only hadn't he told her, he'd never told anyone.

"My mom broke that day." He stared down at their clasped hands, began massaging her hand as if it weren't connected to her, just an object to keep himself distracted. "She was great, everything a kid could ask for in a single mom, but she's never even dated again. 'No point,' is all she says to anyone who asks. I swore as a kid that I'd never be with a serving soldier."

Then he looked up at her. Those deep brown eyes so close and intense. "No one. And I mean no one ever came close to making me break that vow, except you. So I need you to be really sure that you want me in your bed for more than a one-night rehab therapy session. Because to me, it's a hell of a lot more important than that."

# 9

***Lois stood at the*** living room window, lit only by the distant field lights that found their way here, for a long time after she sent Kendall away into the cool spring night. She'd sent him with half a pizza and the best kiss of her life, but she'd sent him nonetheless.

"I don't dare risk hurting you as much as I expect I will," she'd told him. He was too important, though she was unclear how or when that had happened.

He'd tried to protest that he could take care of his own hurt, but she'd refused.

"Time. Give me some time." That's when

he'd hit her with that kiss. It hadn't scorched and burned like last night's. Instead, it had asked and promised. She had wrapped her leg—her missing leg—behind him to keep him close and neither of them had reacted to that. She'd wanted and needed, but she hadn't taken. Hadn't taken him to her bed or taken him on the couch.

Instead, she had shown him the door and, without a word, released him into the night.

From her front window, she could see the airfield lights shining beyond the next set of barracks. Dozens of helicopters were parked there, the more specialized ones tucked safely out of sight in hangars. That's where her heart had been, tucked safely out of sight.

The question she couldn't answer was how safe it would be if it got out.

# 10

***For a week, Lois*** went to the PEB offices to check if there was any information on her paperwork processing. More often than not she met Clara the AW2 advocate for lunch. Clara didn't push anymore. Instead, as they slowly became friends, she told Lois her own story.

"I was part of Team Lioness. We were temporarily attached to Army and Marine units, meaning we were dropped into combat teams without heavy combat training. Our job was to frisk and communicate with the women so as not to violate their religious laws against any man other than their husbands interacting them. You tell me how we go in with a gung-ho Marine team and don't end up in the thick of it."

"Pixie dust? I hear the Pentagon is making that standard issue now."

Clara laughed. "Could have used some. I got this one woman cleared of guns, and she had several. But my teammate hadn't secured this damn big kitchen knife just sitting out in the open. She missed my heart by that much." She raised her artificial arm. Her prosthetic began just below the shoulder. She'd chosen a cosmetic arm controlled by wires to a harness attached to her opposite shoulder. It was good enough that it would have passed for real at a casual glance, if she hadn't chosen a short-sleeved blouse to go with it.

Lois could only admire the ease with which Clara moved through the world. But Lois could never be a paper pusher, nor a hand holder. She was a combat pilot who could no longer fly with her team. The near daily emails they kicked her from the front were both precious and painful. Their lives were going on, and hers had stopped. But they were flying, that was something she'd done for them that they'd never know. Her crew was still up in the air... even if she wasn't.

Lois saw plenty of Clara, but she didn't see much of Kendall. She stayed away from the hangar and simulator building. He, in turn, didn't come calling. It didn't feel as if he was avoiding her so much as giving her space to think.

Damn him for being so blasted decent. It just made her think about him all the more. His compliment, which had rankled at first, had shifted over time. "Didn't want her while she flew," had shifted into the background. "Had almost made him break his own promise to himself," shifted forward.

Why had she never hooked up with him? He was funny, handsome, smart, and a damned fine pilot for a civilian. She had high standards, but he flew past all those easily. Also on the plus side, he was a civilian, so no fraternization issues would have come up.

Over the second week, she eventually reached the conclusion that the reason Lois Lang and Kendall Clark had never become an item was that she was as stupid as a brick.

Which was about how she'd always ranked Clark Kent for never bedding Lois in the movies.

# 11

***Neutral ground again, she*** was waiting outside the main hangar as he returned from a training flight. She'd been building up her walks, stretching the half mile to the PEB offices out to a mile, then two.

For today, she taken the risk and left her cane behind. She'd gone back to a skirt again for the first time since their Stanley and Seafort's date and was relaxing on a bench on the service side of the hangar. The afternoon sun had almost lulled her to sleep by the time he flew back in. Daylight training today.

"Great leg!" he stood in a full flightsuit, his

helmet under one arm, and the lowering sun lighting him up from behind.

"Which one?"

"I'm an engineer."

She laughed, she couldn't help herself. He simply made her feel good about herself. "You done for the day?"

He nodded.

"How about I take you to dinner?" For an answer all he did was smile.

She'd actually cooked. Nothing fancy, but she'd made the lasagna from scratch, except for the red sauce, which was jarred because life really was too short. The post commissary also had some great baguettes, so she'd snagged one and a bag of salad.

The meal hadn't been hurried. At first, they were avoiding that she'd propositioned him and he'd pretty much said he loved her. But soon it fell by the wayside as they each told mom-stories and flying tall tales. Much of the evening had passed before a comfortable silence fell between them.

She stood. "I'm not much for romantic gestures," and she reached out a hand.

Without a word, he rose, scooped her up

in his arms over her cry of protest, and carried her into the bedroom. He neither made a point of nor ignored her leg. Undressing each other was a slow, mutual, and nerve-tingling experience.

And still he didn't address her leg. Not until her skirt was off and little remained—just panties, bra, and prosthesis—did he mention it. He no longer boasted any clothes at all, and she knew she'd been mad to have avoided him for so long. Kendall's body wasn't soldier strong, it was more than that. He had the strength without the overstressed leanness that so often accompanied the military lifestyle. Runs, weight room, constant training made for excellent conditioning and endurance. But the physical stresses that showed so clearly on a soldier—even worse after a forward deployment—were absent from his body. Kendall's physique had all the advantages and none of the drawbacks.

"Show me how," he whispered as he nuzzled her breast, through the bra's fabric.

"Not if it means you're going to stop doing that."

He obliged her until long after that bit of clothing no longer hindered his investigations.

She sat up on the edge of the bed. He sat beside her. When she reached for a buckle, it felt as if she was about to expose herself far more than merely removing her clothes.

Sensing her apprehension, he slid his fingers beneath hers and undid the first one. She guided his hand to the second. With a slight shake and a push, it came free.

He knelt before her. This beautiful, naked, gentle man knelt before her, and slid the leg off. Setting it carefully aside, he peeled off one anti-abrasion sock and then the other.

Lois had never in her life been so exposed or felt so vulnerable. And then he kissed the inside of her bare thigh, and the sensation rocketed into her so hard and sharp that she cried out, not knowing if it was pleasure or pain.

Kendall took his time proving that it was indeed pleasure.

# 12

***A training schedule order.***

Lois hadn't had one of those in a long time.

It was simple, clear, and she had no doubt who was behind it.

*Simulator #3 – 1700 hours*

*Report to Master Sergeant Jake Hamlin.*

She wanted to tell Kendall to go to hell. They'd been lovers for a month, and he'd kept asking her if she wanted to go up for a real flight in an actual Hawk. Kept asking until she'd shut him down hard. It was the closest they'd come to a fight; his impossible calm only making her fears all the worse. She'd shut him down so hard that he'd never brought it up again. Which was good because every mention of flying, especially in her beloved Black Hawk, had cut at her like a knife.

She tried to track him down to tell him to go to hell, but obviously he'd guessed that's what she'd do.

His cell phone went straight to voicemail, and if he was anywhere on post, she sure wasn't finding him.

But the damned training schedule wasn't a request; it was an order. Signed by the battalion commander no less. You didn't refuse an order, no matter how much it pissed you off. That would get her out of the service far faster than the slow-moving Eval Board process. She'd be out on her ass with a dishonorable discharge mere minutes after her court-martial was done and over.

Fine!

At 1659 hours, US Army Captain Lois Lang was sitting in the "up next" chair in the simulator building wearing her ACU fatigues and carrying her scuffed and scratched helmet with the big red "S" on a field of yellow in an irregular pentagon on the side.

Jake climbed down along with some other trainee he'd just put through the wringer. He sauntered over to her, started to smile, and then thought better of it.

For maybe the first time in her life, he straightened up into rigid attention and gave her a parade ground salute.

"We're ready when you are, Captain."

She rose and returned the salute as formally as it had been given.

"I'm so not, Jake. And I want to apologize beforehand for the civilian blood I'm going to be spilling all over the inside of your nice simulator when I get up there. Clark is toast."

"Don't worry, Ma'am. Be glad to clean it up. But I would note one thing before you commit murder."

"Fire away," she pulled on her helmet and began cinching it down.

"Listen to him first. He's as good at what he does as you are at what you do."

"*Did.* Past tense, Jake."

This time he smiled down at her.

"What?"

"Go get him, Superwoman."

And she would. She climbed the stairs, Jake again riding safety behind her—though she felt far less need for it this time—and settled in just as she would for any training flight.

"What's the scenario?" She snapped out as a greeting. Nothing said she had to be polite to a civilian, even if he was sharing her bed and made her feel like Venus despite her missing limb.

"You have a choice of two, Captain." Kendall kept it formal. He was never stupid and would know full well just how pissed she was. "We have a standard Jake torture test."

Jake's Tortures, as they were known far and wide, were notorious. Not many pilots survived those. The simulator had six major categories of weather and eighteen of failures; some of which had dozens of options. There were technical and moral challenges. Engine fires and very hot targets, copilot bleeding out versus terrorist getting away with it. You never knew what was coming, and there was always something new.

"The second one?"

"It's one that I designed, Lois. Just for you.

Based on a real flight tape." The tone of his voice got to her. He knew her so well, had gotten past every shield she'd ever had, ever thrown up. Over the last month, he'd convinced her that maybe, just maybe she could find a way to live in the "new life" without hating it so much. Without having to work every day to find the positive, the upside.

*Designed it just for me.* In the soft, personal tone that he didn't even use when they had exhausted each other by pushing the bounds of sex to new limits. No, it was that quiet, gentle tone each time she awoke from the nightmare, and he held her and told her everything would be all right.

*Damn him!*

She took a deep breath, dropped her hands on the controls, and let the breath out slowly. Then a nod to, "Bring it on." She didn't trust herself to speak.

*NSDQ.*

*NSDQ.*

*Night Stalkers Don't Quit.* She began her mantra. *NSD—*

Unholy hell broke out all around her. Her helmet's tactical display reported a dozen sources of gunfire. The covering fire from the DAP Hawk circling above them wouldn't be enough for much longer.

A technical came around the far side of the crashed Little Bird, clearing a boulder in a four-wheel slide that was the only reason the gunner couldn't get a bead on her fast enough. She could see in her night vision the big twin barrels of a Russian ZU-23 anti-aircraft gun mounted on the truck's bed slowly swinging to aim at her cockpit. It fired one-inch shells that would punch through the Hawk's armor as if it wasn't even there.

Even as she cried out his name and the direction, Hi-Gear took it out, gunner, gun, and then the vehicle. The fireball was blinding through the windscreen, the night-vision gear temporarily overloaded.

"Ten," one of the medics called out as he raced back from the crashed Little Bird.

Still blinking hard, she couldn't see anything yet, she began counting down the seconds. At five, she pulled the collective up to get a low hover. It would also raise the blade tips almost two feet, making the medic's passage beneath the spinning disk that much safer.

At zero, everyone was aboard and at plus-three seconds she got the signal and she was gone.

Punching out through her own dust cloud, her adrenaline pumping high and hot, she slammed into the first turn.

Then she saw it.

This time, before the warning systems, before she had in reality, Lois spotted the spark of heat from the RPG's firing. Even if she'd seen it that early in reality, the only way to save her Black Hawk would have been to roll right and up.

If she did, the RPG would have blown into the rear cargo bay, killing her entire crew. Had she seen it in time, her answer would have been the same: to hold the turn.

It played out, but she was no longer connected, no longer in control. She simply watched the helo's recorder play out the sequence of events.

The hit to Engine One.

Kendall pulling the Fire Suppress T-handle at the same moment Dusty had.

She could have belly-flopped into the rocks, killed most of her crew and possibly—she looked again at the rocks—probably walked away.

But her decision, the only real choice—at least for her—was to turn her own side of the helicopter into the cliff wall and to keep her foot down on the right pedal to kick the tail and the rear cargo bay up into the air, over that deadly line of boulders. She did so again, not that it would change how the tape played out.

Again, she watched as the helicopter nosed in and tumbled. Could feel the searing pain once again in her right leg. Could remember pushing and pushing against the pain as they rolled, even after there was no longer any pedal to push against or any foot to push with.

The video came to a stop. The machine rocking once, twice, and then dying from the abuse.

Dusty must have pulled the flight recorder cartridge during the evac.

She'd never seen it before, hadn't thought about it. The review board had exonerated her long before she was out of the drugs enough to care. She'd awoken to a Purple Heart and a Silver Star Medal for valor. She'd known why, she just didn't know how anyone else knew.

This probably meant her crew knew, and that's why they stayed in such close touch. She'd saved their lives at such a cost to herself.

"It was the only choice." Her voice was hoarse and scratchy as she confirmed what she'd always known.

"It was the damned bravest thing I've ever seen," Jake Hamlin said gruffly from behind them. "An honor and a privilege, Captain. An honor and a privilege." Once again, he left her alone with Kendall in the cockpit of the simulator.

Her heart was calm. The adrenaline comedown wasn't bad as such things went.

"Hell of a risk there, Clark. Sending your girlfriend back on that flight."

"Hell of a risk," he agreed quietly, "to do that to the woman you love." He'd said he loved her before, but never with that roughness of honesty she couldn't deny.

"Why? I mean we had a good thing going. Why did you risk it? Trying to cure me of my nightmares?" And she did love him back. But that didn't mean she could say it.

"No. Trying to cure you of your stupid-ass idea of leaving the service. Your heart would die without it. Look at how much you have to give. Just because you can't fly combat, doesn't mean you can't train others to make those hard choices when they have to."

She kept her silence. It was a big idea. A huge one and it would take a bit of getting used to.

He filled the silence that she couldn't. "I've been flying training missions in this box and through the Pacific Northwest for five years now. Maybe one in fifty could have done that maneuver even if they tried. Maybe one in a thousand would have made that choice. You saved your entire crew and all three casualties, Lois. Every one of them. You really are Superwoman. You've got to know that's worth teaching."

Lois began shutting down the flight controls, resetting the simulator so that it was no longer a crashed helicopter on a field of boulders half a world away.

Kendall was right. She was going to have to sit down with Clara and get her foot in the door with AW2, so to speak.

"You really love me enough to risk losing me? For my own good?"

"I do."

Lois pulled off her helmet and rested it on the joystick of the cyclic, brushing at the scuffs and scratches across the Superwoman logo. She turned to look at Kendall for the first time since she'd entered the simulator. Saw that, as Superman always would, he spoke absolute truth.

"Of course, I had an ace in the hole." His deep voice was a caress.

"What was that?"

He tapped her helmet. Not the logo, but the heavy block letters she'd had painted beneath it.

How could she help but be madly in love with a man who understood her better than she understood herself? Well, if he'd risk that much for her, she could do no less for him.

Lois now knew that Kendall deserved only one answer. An answer that she would give gladly, now and on the altar.

It was a promise to last them a lifetime.

"NSDQ."

# Afterword

***This story was inspired*** by "CNN Top 10 Hero of 2013" Dale Beatty and his battle buddy John Gallina. After volunteers built a home for double-amputee Dale (for whom the Soleus Tactical feet were designed), they cofounded Purple Heart Homes—a non-profit organization that has built or remodeled dozens of homes for disabled veterans. More information at:

www.purplehearthomesusa.org

# About the Author

***M. L. Buchman has*** over 50 novels and 30 short stories in print. His military romantic suspense books have been named Barnes & Noble and NPR "Top 5 of the year" and twice *Booklist* "Top 10 of the Year," placing two titles on their "Top 101 Romances of the Last 10 Years" list. He has been nominated for the Reviewer's Choice Award for "Top 10 Romantic Suspense of the Year" by *RT Book Reviews* and was a 2016 RWA RITA finalist. In addition to romance, he also writes thrillers, fantasy, and science fiction.

In among his career as a corporate project

manager he has: rebuilt and single-handed a fifty-foot sailboat, both flown and jumped out of airplanes, and designed and built two houses. Somewhere in there he also bicycled solo around the world.

He is now making his living as a full-time writer on the Oregon Coast with his beloved wife. He is constantly amazed at what you can do with a degree in Geophysics. You may keep up with his writing by subscribing to his newsletter at www.mlbuchman.com.

*If you enjoyed this story, you might also enjoy:*

## Target of the Heart (excerpt)
## -a Night Stalkers 5E novel-

***Major Pete Napier hovered*** his MH-47G Chinook helicopter ten kilometers outside of Lhasa, Tibet and a mere two inches off the tundra. A mixed action team of Delta Force and The Activity—the slipperiest intel group on the planet—flung themselves aboard.

The additional load sent an infinitesimal shift in the cyclic control in his right hand. The hydraulics to close the rear loading ramp hummed through the entire frame of the massive helicopter. By the time his crew chief could reach forward to slap an "all secure" signal against his shoulder, they were already ten feet up and fifty out. That was enough altitude. He kept the nose down as he clawed for speed in the thin air at eleven thousand feet.

"Totally worth it," one of the D-boys announced as soon as he was on the Chinook's internal intercom.

He'd have to remember to tell that to the two Black Hawks flying guard for him…when they were in a friendly country and could risk a radio transmission. This deep inside China—or rather Chinese-held territory as the CIA's mission-briefing spook had insisted on calling it—radios attracted attention and were only used to avoid imminent death and destruction.

"Great, now I just need to get us out of this alive."

"Do that, Pete. We'd appreciate it."

He wished to hell he had a stealth bird like the one that had gone into bin Laden's compound. But the one that had crashed during that raid had been blown up. Where there was one, there were always two, but the second had gone back into hiding as thoroughly as if it had never existed. He hadn't heard a word about it since.

The Tibetan terrain was amazing, even if all he could see of it was the monochromatic green of night vision. And blackness. The largest city in Tibet lay a mere ten kilometers away and they were flying over barren wilderness. He could crash out here and no one would know for decades unless some yak herder stumbled upon them. Or were yaks in Mongolia? He was a corn-fed, white boy from Colorado, what did he know about Tibet? Most of the countries he'd flown into on black ops missions he'd only seen at night anyway.

While moving very, very fast.

Like now.

The inside of his visor was painted with overlapping readouts. A pre-defined terrain map, the best that modern satellite imaging could build made the first layer. This wasn't some crappy, on-line, look-at-a-picture-of-your-house display. Someone had a pile of dung outside their goat pen? He could see it, tell you how high it was, and probably say if they were pygmy goats or full-size LaManchas by the size of their shit-pellets if he zoomed in.

On top of that were projected the forward-looking infrared camera images. The FLIR imaging gave him a real-time overlay, in case someone had put an addition onto their goat shed since the last satellite pass, or parked their tractor across his intended flight path.

His nervous system was paying autonomic attention to that combined landscape. He also compensated for the thin air at altitude as he instinctively chose when to start his climb over said goat shed or his swerve around it.

It was the third layer, the tactical display that had most of his attention. At least he and the two Black Hawks flying escort on him were finally on the move.

To insert this deep into Tibet, without passing over Bhutan or Nepal, they'd had to add wingtanks on the Black Hawks' hardpoints where he'd much rather have a couple banks of

Hellfire missiles. Still, they had 20mm chain guns and the crew chiefs had miniguns which was some comfort.

While the action team was busy infiltrating the capital city and gathering intelligence on the particularly brutal Chinese assistant administrator, he and his crews had been squatting out in the wilderness under a camouflage net designed to make his helo look like just another god-forsaken Himalayan lump of granite.

Command had determined that it was better for the helos to wait on site through the day than risk flying out and back in. He and his crew had stood shifts on guard duty, but none of them had slept. They'd been flying together too long to have any new jokes, so they'd played a lot of cribbage. He'd long ago ruled no gambling on a mission, after a fistfight had broken out about a bluff hand that cost a Marine three hundred and forty-seven dollars. Marines hated losing to Army no matter how many times it happened. They'd had to sit on him for a long time before he calmed down.

Tonight's mission was part of an on-going campaign to discredit the Chinese "presence" in Tibet on the international stage—as if occupying the country the last sixty years didn't count toward ruling, whether invited or not. As usual, there was a crucial vote coming up at the U.N.—that, as usual, the Chinese could be guaranteed to ignore. However, the ever-hopeful CIA was in a hurry to make sure that any damaging information that they could validate was disseminated as thoroughly as possible prior to the vote.

Not his concern.

His concern was, were they going to pass over some Chinese sentry post at their top speed of a hundred and ninety-six miles an hour? The sentries would then call down a couple Shenyang J-16 jet fighters that could hustle along at Mach 2 to fry his sorry ass. He knew there was a pair of them parked at Lhasa along with some older gear that would be just as effective against his three helos.

"Don't suppose you could get a move on, Pete?"

"Eat shit, Nicolai!" He was a good man to have as a copilot. Pete knew he was holding on too tight, and Nicolai knew that a joke was the right way to ease the moment.

He, Nicolai, and the four pilots in the two Black Hawks had a long way to go tonight and he'd never make it if he stayed so tight on the controls that he could barely maneuver. Pete eased off and felt his fingers tingle with the rush of returning blood. They dove down into gorges and followed them as long as they dared. They hugged cliff walls at every opportunity to decrease their radar profile. And they climbed.

That was the true danger—they would be up near the helos' limits when they crossed over the backbone of the Himalayas in their rush for India. The air was so rarefied that they burned fuel at a prodigious rate. Their reserve didn't allow for any extended battles while crossing the border…not for any battle at all really.

# # #

It was pitch dark outside her helicopter when Captain Danielle Delacroix stamped on the left rudder pedal while giving the big Chinook right-directed control on the cyclic. It tipped her most of the way onto her side, but let her continue in a straight line. A Chinook's rotors were sixty feet across—front to back they overlapped to make the spread a hundred feet long. By cross-controlling her bird to tip it, she managed to execute a straight line between two mock pylons only thirty feet apart. They were made of thin cloth so they wouldn't down the helo if you sliced one—she was the only trainee to not have cut one yet.

At her current angle of attack, she took up less than a half-rotor of width, just twenty-four feet. That left her nearly three feet to either side, sufficient as she was moving at under a hundred knots.

The training instructor sitting beside her in the copilot's seat didn't react as she swooped through the training course at Fort Campbell, Kentucky. Only child of a single mother, she was used to providing her own feedback loops, so she didn't expect anything else. Those who expected outside validation rarely survived the SOAR induction testing, never mind the two years of training that followed.

As a loner kid, Danielle had learned that self-motivated congratulations and fun were much easier to come by than external ones. She'd spent innumerable hours deep in her mind as a pre-teen superheroine. At twenty-nine she was well on her way to becoming a real life one, though Helo-girl had never been a character she'd thought of in her youth.

External validation or not, after two years of training with the U.S. Army's 160th Special Operations Aviation Regiment she was ready for some action. At least *she* was convinced that she was. But the trainers of Fort Campbell, Kentucky had not signed off on anyone in her trainee class yet. Nor had they given any hint of when they might.

She ducked ten tons of racing Chinook under a bridge and bounced into a vertical climb to clear the power line on the far side. Like a ride on the toboggan at Terrassee Dufferin during *Le Carnaval de Québec,* only with five thousand horsepower at her fingertips. Using her Army signing bonus—the first money in her life that was truly hers—to attend *Le Carnaval* had been her one trip back to her birthplace since her mother took them to America when she was ten.

To even apply to SOAR required five years of prior military rotorcraft experience. She had applied after seven years because of a chance encounter—or rather what she'd thought was a chance encounter at the time.

Captain Justin Roberts had been a top Chinook pilot, the one who had convinced her to switch from her beloved Black Hawk and try out the massive twin-rotor craft. One flight and she'd been a goner, begging her commander until he gave in and let her cross over to the new platform. Justin had made the jump from the 10th Mountain Division to the 160th SOAR not long after that.

Then one night she'd been having pizza in Watertown, New York a couple miles off the 10th's base at Fort Drum.

"Danielle?" Justin had greeted her with the surprise of finding a good friend in an unexpected place. Danielle had liked Justin—even if he was a too-tall, too-handsome cowboy and completely knew it. But "good friend" was unusual for Danielle, with anyone, and Justin came close.

"Captain Roberts," as a dry greeting over the top edge of her Suzanne Brockmann novel didn't faze him in the slightest.

"Mind if I join ya?" A question he then answered for himself by sliding into the opposite seat and taking a slice of her pizza. She been thinking of taking the leftovers back to base, but that was now an idle thought.

"Are you enjoying life in SOAR?" she did her best to appear a normal, social human, a skill she'd learned by rote. *Greeting someone you knew after a time apart? Ask a question about them.* "They treating you well?"

"Whoo-ee, you have no idea, Danielle," his voice was smooth as…well, always…so she wouldn't think about it also sounding like a pickup line. He was beautiful, but didn't interest her; the outgoing ones never did.

"Tell me." *Men love to talk about themselves, so let them.*

And he did. But she'd soon forgotten about her novel, and would have forgotten the pizza if he hadn't reminded her to eat.

His stories shifted from intriguing to fascinating. There was a world out there that she'd been only peripherally aware of. The Night Stalkers of the 160th SOAR weren't simply better helicopter pilots, they were the most highly-trained and best-equipped ones on the planet. Their missions were pure razor's edge and black-op dark.

He'd left her with a hundred questions and enough interest to fill out an application to the 160th. Being a decent guy, Justin even paid for the pizza after eating half.

The speed at which she was rushed into testing told her that her meeting with Justin hadn't been by chance and that she owed him more than half a pizza next time they met. She'd asked after him a couple of times since she'd made it past the qualification exams—and the examiners' brutal interviews that had left her questioning her sanity, never mind her ability.

"Justin Roberts is presently deployed, ma'am," was the only response she'd ever gotten.

Now that she was through training—almost, had to be soon, didn't it?—Danielle realized that was probably less of an evasion and more likely to do with the brutal op tempo the Night Stalkers maintained. The SOAR 1st Battalion had just won the coveted Lt. General Ellis D. Parker awards for Outstanding Combat Aviation Battalion *and* Aviation Battalion of the Year. They'd been on deployment every single day of the last year, actually of the last decade-plus since 9/11.

The very first Special Forces boots on the ground in Afghanistan were delivered that October by the Night Stalkers and nothing had slacked off since. Justin might be in the 5th battalion D company, but they were just as heavily assigned as the 1st.

Part of their training had included tours in Afghanistan. But unlike any of their prior deployments, these were brief, intense, and then they'd be back in the States pushing to integrate their new skills.

SOAR needed her training to end and so did she.

Danielle was ready for the job, in her own, inestimable opinion. But she wasn't going to get there until the trainers signed off that she'd reached fully mission-qualified proficiency.

The Fort Campbell training course was never set up the same from one flight to the next, but it always had a time limit. The time would be short and they didn't tell you what it was. So she drove the Chinook for all it was worth like Regina Jaquess waterskiing her way to U.S. Ski Team Female Athlete of the Year.

The Night Stalkers were a damned secretive lot, and after two years of training, she understood why. With seven years flying for the 10th, she'd thought she was good.

She'd been repeatedly lauded as one of the top pilots at Fort Drum.

The Night Stalkers had offered an education in what it really meant to fly. In the two years of training, she'd flown more hours than in the seven years prior, despite two deployments to Iraq. And spent more time in the classroom than her life-to-date accumulated flight hours.

But she was ready now. It was *très viscérale,* right down in her bones she could feel it. The Chinook was as much a part of her nervous system as breathing.

Too bad they didn't build men the way they built the big Chinooks—especially the MH-47G which were built specifically to SOAR's requirements. The aircraft were steady, trustworthy, and the most immensely powerful helicopters deployed in the U.S. Army—what more could a girl ask for? But finding a superhero man to go with her superhero helicopter was just a fantasy for a lonely teenage girl.

She dove down into a canyon and slid to

a hover mere inches over the reservoir inside the thirty-second window laid out on the flight plan.

Danielle resisted a sigh. She was ready for something to happen and to happen soon.

# # #

Pete's Chinook and his two escort Black Hawks crossed into the mountainous province of Sikkim, India ten feet over the glaciers and still moving fast. It was an hour before dawn, they'd made it out of China while it was still dark.

"Twenty minutes of fuel remaining," Nicolai said it like a personal challenge when they hit the border.

"Thanks, I never would have noticed."

It had been a nail-biting tradeoff: the more fuel he burned, the more easily he climbed due to the lighter load. The more he climbed, the faster he burned what little fuel remained.

Safe in Indian airspace he climbed hard as Nicolai counted down the minutes remaining, burning fuel even faster than he had been while crossing the mountains of southern Tibet. They caught up with the U.S. Air Force

HC-130P Combat King refueling tanker with only ten minutes of fuel left.

"Ram that bitch," Nicolai called out.

Pete extended the refueling probe which reached only a few feet beyond the forward edge of the rotor blade and drove at the basket trailing behind the tanker on its long hose.

He nailed it on the first try despite the fluky winds. Striking the valve in the basket with over four hundred pounds of pressure, a clamp snapped over the refueling probe and Jet A fuel shot into his tanks.

His helo had the least fuel due to having the most men aboard, so he was first in line. His Number Two picked up the second refueling basket trailing off the other wing of the Combat King. Thirty seconds and three hundred gallons later and he was breathing much more easily.

"Ah," Nicolai sighed. "It is better than the sex," his thick Russian accent only ever surfaced in this moment or in a bar while picking up women.

"Hey, Nicolai," Nicky the Greek called over the intercom from his crew chief position seated behind Pete. "Do you make love in Russian?"

A question Pete had always been careful to avoid.

"For you, I make special exception." That got a laugh over the system.

Which explained why Pete always kept his mouth shut at this moment.

"The ladies, Nicolai? What about the ladies?" Alfie the portside gunner asked.

"Ah," he sighed happily as he signaled that the other choppers had finished their refueling and formed up to either side, "the ladies love the Russian. They don't need to know I grew up in Maryland and I learn my great-great-grandfather's native tongue at the University called Virginia."

He sounded so pleased that Pete wished he'd done the same rather than study Japanese and Mandarin.

Another two hours of—thank god—straight-and-level flight at altitude through the breaking dawn and they landed on the aircraft carrier awaiting them in the Bay of Bengal. India had agreed to turn a blind eye as long as the Americans never actually touched their soil.

Once standing on the deck—and the worst

of the kinks had been worked out—he pulled his team together: six pilots and seven crew chiefs.

"Honor to serve!" He saluted them sharply.

"Hell yeah!" They shouted in response and saluted in turn. It was their version of spiking the football in the end zone.

A petty officer in a bright green vest appeared at his elbow, "Follow me please, sir." He pointed toward the Navy-gray command structure that towered above the carrier's deck.

The Commodore of the entire carrier group was waiting for him just outside the entrance. Not a good idea to keep a One-Star waiting, so he waved at the team.

"See you in the mess for dinner," he shouted to the crew over the noise of an F-18 Hornet fighter jet trapping on the #2 wire. After two days of surviving on MREs while squatting on the Tibetan tundra, he was ready for a steak, a burger, a mountain of pasta, whatever. Or maybe all three.

The green escorted him across the hazards of the busy flight deck. Pete had kept his helmet on to buffer the noise, but even at that he winced as another Hornet fired up and was flung aloft by the catapult.

"Orders, Major Napier," the Commodore handed him a folded sheet the moment he arrived. "Hate to lose you."

The Commodore saluted, which Pete automatically returned before looking down at the sheet of paper in his hands. The man was gone before the import of Pete's orders slammed in.

A different green-clad deckhand showed up with Pete's duffle bag and began guiding him toward a loading C-2 Greyhound twin-prop airplane. It was parked number two for the launch catapult, close behind the raised jet-blast deflector.

His crew, being led across in the opposite direction to return to the berthing decks below, looked at him aghast.

"Stateside," was all he managed to gasp out as they passed.

A stream of foul cursing followed him from behind. Their crew was tight. Why the hell was Command breaking it up?

And what in the name of fuck-all had he done to deserve this?

He glanced at the orders again as he stumbled up the Greyhound's rear ramp and crash landed into a seat.

Training rookies?

It was worse than a demotion.

This was punishment.

*This and other titles are available at fine retailers everywhere.*

## Other works by M.L. Buchman

### The Night Stalkers

**Main Flight**

*The Night Is Mine*
*I Own the Dawn*
*Wait Until Dark*
*Take Over at Midnight*
*Light Up the Night*
*Bring On the Dusk*
*By Break of Day*

**White House Holiday**

*Daniel's Christmas*
*Frank's Independence Day*
*Peter's Christmas*
*Zachary's Christmas*
*Roy's Independence Day*

**and the Navy**

*Christmas at Steel Beach*
*Christmas at Peleliu Cove*

**5E**

*Target of the Heart*
*Target Lock on Love*

### Firehawks

**Main Flight**

*Pure Heat*
*Full Blaze*
*Hot Point*
*Flash of Fire*

**Smokejumpers**

*Wildfire at Dawn*

*Wildfire at Larch Creek*

*Wildfire on the Skagit*

**Delta Force**

*Target Engaged*

*Heart Strike*

**Angelo's Hearth**

*Where Dreams are Born*

*Where Dreams Reside*

*Maria's Christmas Table*

*Where Dreams Unfold*

*Where Dreams Are Written*

**Eagle Cove**

*Return to Eagle Cove*

*Recipe for Eagle Cove*

*Longing for Eagle Cove*

*Keepsake for Eagle Cove*

**Deities Anonymous**

*Cookbook from Hell: Reheated*

*Saviors 101*

**Dead Chef Thrillers**

*Swap Out!*

*One Chef!*

*Two Chef!*

**SF/F Titles**

*Nara*

*Monk's Maze*

*The Me and Elsie Chronicles*

*Newsletter signup at:*
*www.mlbuchman.com*

Made in the USA
Middletown, DE
21 December 2016